SOUL DESIRE

L. A. WEATHERLY

Barrington Stoke

First published in 2014 in Great Britain by
Barrington Stoke Ltd
18 Walker Street, Edinburgh, EH3 7LP

www.barringtonstoke.co.uk

ISBN: 978-1-78112-361-4

Printed in China by Leo

To Julie, with love

How can you miss someone you've never met?

❧ 1 ❧

Have you ever had a dream that you didn't want to end? A dream so full of happiness, it makes you smile even as you sleep? You want to stay in it forever. Then you wake up. You try to hold on to the dream, but you can't stop it slipping away – fading into nothing.

You lie in bed and you feel so alone. All you want to do is cry.

That's happened to me more times than I can count. But this time it's not a dream. The boy whose hand I'm holding is real. His fingers are warm and firm in mine. As we walk down the dusty track, his profile looks strong against the starry sky.

At last we've found each other.

We're in the grounds of an old house. I can feel it behind us, as if it's watching us. Just before the gate comes into view, I shiver and stop short.

If we take one more step, we will see the gate. We'll find out whose time we're in.

You see, Nate and I are from different times. Our whole lives, we've longed for one another, without even knowing each other's name. We've shared the same dreams at night, we've haunted each other's thoughts ... but we only just met today. It's all because of this house. We somehow found a time here where we could meet. A time between times.

And now, at last, we're in the same time ... but whose?

The night breeze ruffles Nate's sandy hair as he looks down at me. "Iris, what is it?" he asks.

I lick my lips. They feel dry.

"I don't know," I say. I stare at the shadows around the gate. Why am I so nervous? Nate and I are together now. That's all that matters.

But I can't shake the feeling that something is very wrong.

'You're being stupid,' I tell myself. I push away my worry. "I'm fine," I say out loud.

I see the look in Nate's brown eyes and I relax a little. They're so full of concern. "Are you sure?" he says.

I nod. "Let's go."

Nate doesn't move. "Wait," he says. "There's something I need to do first."

"There is?"

"Yes. It's very important."

He puts his hands on my face and leans his head down. We kiss. I'll never get tired of the feel of Nate's lips on mine. Not ever. I wrap my arms around his neck as he pulls me close.

The heat of our mouths melts me. When we pull apart my heart is racing. I still can't believe that Nate and I have found each other. From the look on Nate's face, he feels the same way.

He clears his throat and touches my long, dark hair. "You know ... I'm kind of glad I came to this old house today," he says.

I smile. "Only 'kind of'?"

He pretends to think about it. "'Fairly'?"

I shrug and act bored. "Fine, that makes two of us. I'm kind of, fairly glad that I came here today, too."

Nate grins and kisses me again, a soft kiss this time. He puts his arm around me and we start walking. The moon comes out from behind a wisp of clouds.

The gate comes into view.

It's old ... but it still looks sturdy. I bite my lip. In my own time, the gate is almost falling down.

Nate lets out a relieved breath. Then he darts a look at me. "I'm sorry," he says.

He means he's sorry that we're in his time, and not mine. That's what he wanted. Maybe he's sorry for that, too.

"Don't be sorry," I tell him. My voice sounds faint. I stare at the gate and try to get my head around the fact that I'm in 1922. My skin prickles as I think about all the things Nate and I will have to live through. The Great Depression. World War II. Nate doesn't know – I haven't told him any of that.

But my time has its own problems. At least Nate will be with his family now. And ... I guess I'll be with his family, too. I have nowhere else to go in this time.

Only – what if his parents don't want me there?

We're at the gate. Nate can tell I'm worried. He takes me by the shoulders and turns me to face him. "It's all right," he says. "Everything will be fine, Iris. I promise you."

"I know," I say. Nate's as stubborn as I am – we will be together, no matter what. Even so, the next few hours might not be much fun.

I try to laugh. "Come on," I say. "We'd better find out what your parents think about you bringing a girl from the future home."

Nate winces and rubs his chin. "Um … I don't think we'll tell them that part."

"Good idea."

Before he can reply, a high, shrieking laugh comes on the wind.

I flinch and spin back towards the house. Nate jumps in front of me, as if to protect me – but there's nothing there. Just the trees, and the shadows. We stare wide-eyed at each other.

"Maybe – maybe it was just a bird," I say. But I know it wasn't.

Nate's jaw is hard. "Let's get out of here," he says. I can tell he's thinking the same thing as I am. What if Sybil, the evil spirit who wanted to keep us apart, isn't really dead after all?

I feel cold all over. Nate and I climb the gate as fast as we can. At the top, we swing our legs over.

Even at a time like this, I can't help watching the way Nate moves. His body is so firm – so sure of itself. I bet that in 1922, all the things I want to do with him are frowned upon.

Nate glances over at me and I go warm. I know he feels the same way about me – that he wants the same things I do.

"I love you, you know," he says in a low voice.

I swallow hard. "I know. I love you, too."

As we climb down the other side, Nate reaches out a hand to help me to the ground. I don't need help, but I take his hand anyway. I never want to let it go.

'Sybil will not keep us apart,' I think. 'Not even if she is still alive. I won't let her.'

Nate squeezes my fingers. "Ready?" he says, and I nod. At the same time, we hop to the ground.

The world seems to explode.

There's a bright flash. I cry out and fall on to my side. My skull feels like an axe is chopping into it – over and over. I scream, holding my head and rolling back and forth. The world's gone white with pain – like something is being ripped away from me.

Then it stops.

I shudder as I sit up. I'm breathless. The sun is out now – it's a hot summer day.

"Nate?" I say.

He's not here. I scramble to my feet. "Nate!" I shout. I look wildly around me. There's no sign of him. But he was right there, holding my hand!

I jump back as a car passes on the road and honks its horn. It's one of those funny, old-time ones. I'm still in 1922. I grab the bars of the gate, ready to climb it again and look for Nate.

But I don't climb. I stand and stare down the track at the house. All of a sudden I feel faint.

It's not the same house.

2

The house that Nate and I knew was very grand, but even when it was old and abandoned, it had a friendly feel. This one looks like something out of a horror film. It's tall and grey, with two small towers at the top.

I gape at it. The other house was the one place Nate and I could meet, even in our different times. If it's not the same anymore …

Panic grips me. "Nate!" I yell. "Are you here?"

The gate looks brand new – it opens when I try it. I race down the track and jog up the steps. Somebody lives here. There's another old-fashioned car parked in the drive, and everything is very tidy.

I feel dizzy. I press the doorbell and then hug myself. 'Please, please,' I think. 'Nate has *got* to be here.'

A woman comes to the door. She has brown hair pulled back in a bun and her dress is kind of baggy, with a long waist.

She stares at me. I stare back.

"Is – is Nate here?" I stammer.

"*Who?*" the woman snaps. She looks me up and down. I remember that Nate thought I was dressed as a boy when he first saw me. My jeans and T-shirt must seem really weird to this woman in 1922.

"Nate," I say again. Then my heart sinks – I don't know his last name! Or whether 'Nate' is short for 'Nathan' or 'Nathaniel'. I know him inside and out ... but don't know those basic facts.

The woman's voice is cold. "There's no one here by that name."

I lick my lips. "Are you sure? He's 17, about six feet tall, and –"

"And he's *not here*," she breaks in. "I suggest that you leave now, young lady."

I'm starting to hate her. And more than that, I'm starting to feel very scared. Over her shoulder, I can see the inside of the house. It has totally changed too.

When I first came here, Nate and I were still in different times. I couldn't see him, but I could *feel* him – hear him calling me.

Now there's nothing. Wherever Nate is … it isn't here.

"All right," I say. My voice sounds faint. "I'm sorry I bothered you."

☙☙

I don't know where to go after that. I walk down the road. My backpack is gone – Nate had it when we jumped off the gate. But a lost bag is the least of my worries. After a while I lean against a tree and try to think.

Oh God, what's happened? Where's Nate?

My head pounds as I think of that high, shrieking laugh again. The day is hot, but then … I feel a shiver, as if something is watching me. I snap my head around to look behind me. Nothing.

'OK, Iris, think!' I rub my arms, and then I remember something. Nate said that he doesn't live far from here. Maybe he just got zapped to his home, somehow. He could be looking for me right now.

I want this to be true so much that it hurts. I keep walking – and soon I start to see other homes. Some are like small farms, with chickens and horses. Hills rise up behind them. Nate told me how much he loves hiking in the mountains. I can see why, if he lives around here.

Nate.

I cross my arms tight around my chest as I walk. I *will* find him. It's going to be all right.

Then I stop. There's a metal, sliding sound coming towards me. I've never heard anything like it. For a second I hesitate. What *is* it?

When I turn a bend and see, I almost laugh. It's just a girl wearing old-fashioned metal roller skates. As she glides towards me the wheels scrape against the paved road. She looks so serious, like she's really got to concentrate.

"Hi," I call out when she gets close.

The girl's around 12 and has on a blue dress. Her long blond hair is in plaits. She comes to a halt in front of me.

"Hello," she says. Her forehead furrows as she studies me. "Why are you dressed like that?"

I go still as I study her, too. Her brown eyes are the same colour as Nate's. And her hair's the same as his – a dark, sandy blond. I remember what Nate said about his family. "I've got parents – a little sister named Ruth."

My fists clench. I can hardly get the words out. "Are you Ruth?" I ask.

Her eyebrows shoot up. "Yes! How did you know?"

My smile must be stretching across my whole face. "I know your brother," I tell her. The words tumble out. "Is he home? He's probably looking for me ..."

I trail off. Ruth's staring at me as if I'm crazy. She shakes her head.

"Sorry," she says. "I haven't got a brother."

❧ 3 ❧

For a second I can't believe what I've heard. "But you *do*!" I burst out. "Ruth, I *know* you do. His name's Nate, and he looks just like you!"

"Nate?" she repeats. Her cheeks go a little pale.

"Yes!" I grab her arm without thinking. "Please, you've got to take me to him, right now!"

"I don't know what you're talking about!" she gasps. She tries to pull away. "I don't have any brothers *or* sisters. You can ask my parents!"

All of a sudden I realise how tight I'm holding her arm. I let go, but can't stop staring at her. "I – I don't understand," I whisper. "You really don't have a brother?"

Ruth shakes her head. Her eyes are the size of dinner plates. "No, I really don't. I'm an only child."

It feels like a hammer is splitting my skull. I go to the side of the road and sink down on to the grass. "I'm going insane," I murmur. I grip my head in both hands. "Nate, where *are* you?"

Ruth hesitates and then wheels over and sits down beside me. "Why did you think I have a brother?" she asks.

I shake my head. "It's … a long story."

She shrugs and takes the skates off her shoes. "I've got time."

"I'm not sure I do," I say. I'm not sure of much at all anymore – and anything to do with time is a *big* problem.

Ruth eyes my clothes again. "Where are you from, anyway?"

"Texas," I tell her. It's the truth, only in about a hundred years from now.

She looks like she gets it all of a sudden. "Oh!" she says. "You're a cowgirl! *That's* why you're wearing jeans!"

If I wasn't so worried, I'd laugh. "Kind of," I say.

'Is Nate in my time, now?' I wonder. 'Did we swap times, somehow?' But that wouldn't explain why things are so different here. I look at Ruth again – her brown eyes and blond hair. This *has* to be the same Ruth who's Nate's sister! Or maybe I've got it all wrong.

'His parents,' I think. 'I've got to talk to them. Then I'll know.'

I clear my throat. "Ruth, listen ..." I say. "My name's Iris, and I'm lost. Do you think your parents would let me use their phone?"

Then I wonder if people even have phones in 1922. But Ruth jumps to her feet. "Sure," she says. "I bet Mom wouldn't mind. Come on – I don't live far from here."

As Ruth and I walk, I try not to act like I'm worried out of my mind. Ruth swings her skates in one hand. She looks deep in thought. "You know ... it's funny that you thought I had a brother named Nate," she says at last.

My heart skips. "Why?"

"Because I used to pretend I had a big brother named Nate." She goes red. "It was only a game," she mumbles. "But I used to pretend that all the time."

I go cold. If this is true, what does it mean?

Before I can say anything, we reach a ranch-style house. There's a bike on the front porch, and flowers in the yard. The mailbox has the name 'Baxter' on the side in white letters.

"This is it," Ruth says, and runs up the drive.

Inside, we find Ruth's mother in a sunny front room, painting a picture. She covers it up when we come in. Ruth explains who I am. I wince at the word 'cowgirl'. It sounds beyond stupid.

Ruth's mother seems to thinks so, too. She gives me a sharp look. "Thank you, Ruth," she says. "Would you excuse Iris and me for a moment, please?"

When we're alone, she sits me down on the sofa with her. The room's just like Nate described, with a piano in one corner and a cheerful red rug on the floor. There are plants all around, and some kind of record player. It's made of wood and shiny brass, with a wind-up handle and a speaker that looks like a trumpet.

"Now, dear, you're not *really* a cowgirl, are you?" Mrs Baxter asks with a gentle smile.

I'd have known she was Nate's mother anywhere, even with her dark hair. Her eyes are just the same as his – brown and kind. She'll know who Nate is. She *has* to.

"No, I'm not a cowgirl," I tell her. I try to smile. "I'm here because I'm looking for a boy named Nate."

I watch her as I say his name, but she just seems puzzled. "Nate?" she repeats. "I'm sorry, I don't know anyone by that name. Is he around your age?"

My heart plummets. 'This is wrong!' I think. 'This is so, so wrong.'

"Maybe you know him as Nathan," I say in a rush. "Or Nathaniel. He's 17, and he's about six feet tall ..." I go on, describing Nate. I even tell her what he was wearing – tan trousers and a soft white shirt.

"And he has a watch," I finish, feeling desperate. "With a brown leather strap and a round face. Oh, please, you *have* to know him!"

Nate's mother looks over at the covered painting. She opens her mouth and then closes it again. "No," she says, "I don't know him." She presses a hand to her head as if she has a pain there.

I stare at her. I wish I knew what she was thinking. "Are you sure?" I ask.

She sits up straighter. "Yes, I'm sure." Her voice is firm now. "It's just a little odd, that's all."

"What is?"

She gets up and goes over to the painting. She lifts the cover. "Look," she says.

I can't help gasping. The painting is of a boy standing in a garden. He has his hands in his pockets and he's looking right out at the viewer. The boy is Nate, every last bit of him – from his strong shoulders to the look in his eyes.

"That's him!" I cry.

Mrs Baxter covers the painting again. "I'm an artist," she says. "I paint whatever comes to mind. I've painted this boy a lot, for some reason. But he's not a real person."

"He is!" I say. "He should *be* here!"

She gives me a funny look. "Whatever do you mean?"

"This is his house! He –" I'm about to say, 'he's your son' ... when a sudden chill runs over me.

I almost jump. That sense of being watched is back. Something's in this room. Something smug that's enjoying every second of this. I look around me, wild. Is it Sybil? Oh God, why can't she just leave Nate and me alone?

Mrs Baxter touches my arm. "Iris? Are you all right?"

"I'm fine," I say. In fact, I feel dizzy. But at least I didn't tell Mrs Baxter that the boy in the painting is her son. She must think I'm crazy enough already.

Mrs Baxter frowns. "Who *is* this Nate? Why do you need to find him so badly?"

My hands are fists. "I just do."

"Have you tried the police?"

"No!" It comes out sharp. Somehow I know that it would be a very bad idea to talk to the police. What would I even tell them?

Nate's mother studies me for a moment. "My dear, are you in some kind of trouble?" she asks. "Is that why you're dressed like a boy?"

I wince and look down. "I ran away," I admit. "The place I was in was ... not good."

"If you need help ..."

I lick my lips and look at the piano. It has some framed black and white photos on it. Ruth. Nate's mother. A man who must be Nate's father. He looks a little like an older Nate ... only he seems so sad. So does Mrs Baxter, I realise. It's as if she hasn't smiled in a long time.

Nate didn't say anything about sadness. The family he described sounded like they laughed a lot together.

I keep staring at the photos. I don't know how to put all the puzzle pieces together. I just know that I have to do it, or I'll never see Nate again.

"Yes," I tell Mrs Baxter. "I need help."

❧ 4 ❧

I stand at a window and stare out at the hills.

I'm in the Baxters' guest bedroom. It's sunset now – and the hills are the same ones that Nate told me about. "I love looking at them," he'd told me. "The shape is like a sleeping camel. When I was little, I pretended they really *were* one. I called him Rufus."

He'd grinned when I laughed. "It's true," he said. We were sitting in the window seat of the old house, and he took my hand and drew a shape on it with his finger. "Like this," he said. "That's Rufus."

I draw the same shape now with my own finger, the outline of the hills. Rufus the sleeping camel. How could I have imagined a fact like that? How could this *not* be Nate's bedroom?

But it's not. It's a spare room with a high four-poster bed and a lamp with a fringed shade. A mirror in a wooden frame sits on the dresser, beside a silver hairbrush and matching comb. There's not the smallest sign that a teenage boy ever lived here – especially one as messy as Nate claimed to be.

"Well, I like things to be really neat," I'd told him. "I even put my books in order from A to Z."

Nate's mouth had twitched. "Please tell me you're making that up."

"Sorry. Messy rooms make my head hurt." I'd tapped him on the chest. "So you better change your ways, or we'll have some epic fights."

He'd put his arms around me. I could feel his smile against my hair. "Oh, but think of all the fun we'll have making up," he whispered.

I swallow hard. I want to believe that Nate is safe in some other time, but if that was the case, he'd have still grown up here, wouldn't he? Just like I grew up in *my* own time. Instead, Ruth used to imagine a brother named Nate. Her mother doesn't know who he is, but she paints a boy who looks just like him.

It's as if he *should* have grown up here ... but he didn't.

I lean my head against the glass. "Where is he, Rufus?" I whisper to the hills.

Behind me, the bedroom door opens. I turn. It's Nate's mother with a pile of clothes. "I think these might fit you," she says. "You and my sister are about the same size. She keeps some things here."

"Thank you," I say as she puts the clothes on the bed. Dresses, skirts, stockings. Even a pair of shoes with low heels.

Mrs Baxter hesitates as she studies me. "It's so strange, but I feel as if I know you."

I look up. "Really?"

"Or no, that's not quite right. I feel as if I should know you, or *will* know you ..." She gives an uncertain laugh. "Never mind. Why don't you get changed, and we'll have some dinner?" She puts her hand on my arm. "And Iris, you can stay here as long as you like."

After she leaves I try on a skirt and blouse, then study myself in the mirror. The blouse has a long waist and the skirt comes down just past my knees. I could win a Roaring 20s contest with ease.

"I don't care what you wear," Nate had told me. "You look beautiful. No, you look ... stunning."

I frown to hide the fact that I want to cry. I look in the mirror as I pull my hair back in a ponytail with a ribbon – and then I remember that Nate said he'd carved his name on his dresser when he was 10, and got into trouble for it. I gaze down. The wood of the dresser is unmarked.

But for just a second, I know the exact place his carved name should be. I stroke my fingers over the spot. I can almost feel the letters.

A sneering laugh comes from behind me. I jerk my hand away. In the mirror, my grey eyes look wide and startled.

"Is that you, Sybil?" My voice shakes, and I speak louder. I try to sound as tough as I can. "Whatever you've done, change it back – *now*! Then leave us the hell alone!"

No one answers ... because nothing is there.

∞

At dinner, I realise that I haven't seen Nate's father yet. "Will Mr Baxter mind that I'm here?" I ask.

A silence falls. Mrs Baxter forces a smile. "My husband is away a lot. He's on a lecture tour right now. But I'm sure he won't mind."

"Oh," I say. My thoughts are spinning. A lecture tour? Nate said his father was a professor at the university. He made it sound like his dad was home all the time.

So this is something else that's wrong. Nate didn't grow up here, and his father isn't even around.

Ruth eats with one leg folded up under her. She chatters non-stop. "Mom says you're not really a cowgirl," she tells me. "I wish you were! Are you really from Texas? What's it like there?"

"Ruth, don't pester her." Mrs Baxter looks concerned. I bet she's got a good idea of the kind of reasons girls like me run away from home – the kind of things that the creep at my group home tried with me. In 1922 he hasn't even been born yet, but people like him must exist in every time.

I clear my throat. "That's OK," I say.

I tell Ruth about Texas while we eat, but I have to be careful. If I make it sound like I'm not from 1922, they'll think I'm insane. Ruth listens with wide eyes. Even Mrs Baxter seems riveted. I guess in 1922, people don't travel as much.

"And in some places, it's so flat you can see for miles," I tell them. I start to say something else ... and then I stop.

I stare around me at the old-fashioned dining room, with its china cabinet and flowery wallpaper. All of a sudden I can't think why I'm here. Wasn't there some reason? Something important ... Something I needed to find ...

"Iris?" Mrs Baxter says.

I look at her, still confused. Then I see her brown eyes. They're just like someone else's – and it all comes flooding back.

Nate. I grip my fork. How could I have forgotten about him, even for a second? My veins feel like ice, but I try to look calm. "I'm fine," I say. "Just tired, I guess."

I'm not fine – I have a terrible feeling that Nate's in danger, wherever he is. Fear pounds through me.

I've got to help him, only I have no idea how.

❧ 5 ❧

That night I can't let myself fall asleep – because
I don't know what I'll dream. Before, Nate and I
always dreamed about each other. But now ... I
shiver, and hug myself in my borrowed nightie.
What if I *don't* dream of Nate? What would that
mean? I don't want to find out.

"Hang on, Nate," I whisper. He needs help, I
just know it. I've got to do something!

'The old house,' I think in panic. 'It's so
different now. It *must* be the key.'

All of a sudden I decide. I'm going back
there – now, while everyone's asleep. I slip out
of bed and put on the old-fashioned skirt and
blouse, so I won't stand out if anyone sees me.

I creep through the house. The front door's
unlocked. Outside, the night is cool. There's a
full moon. I can see my shadow as I start down

the road. There are a million stars out – more than I've ever seen.

If Nate were here with me, this would be magical. Instead I'm so worried that I feel sick. Plus my neck's tingling again, like someone's watching me. I keep looking over my shoulder, but nothing's there.

"Stay calm, Iris," I mutter to myself.

Soon I come to the old house. Its outline looks even creepier at night, with those two towers etched against the stars. I try the gate but it's locked now. Big surprise.

I go around to the side of the house where the fence is in shadow and I climb over. Everything's so quiet, apart from the hammer of my pulse. I'm sure the woman in the house can hear my every move.

I drop to the ground on the other side. The night air smells like oranges.

OK, now what? I gaze at the house. It looms over me like a giant. The other house seemed to invite me in – this one seems to say, 'Go away, you're not wanted.'

Well, too bad. It's not getting rid of me.

I go to the north-east corner of the house. I'm not sure why. I just feel drawn to it – the same as I always felt drawn to come here to these hills over Los Angeles.

When I reach the house I crouch in the moonlight. I feel tense with hope. I touch the big square stone at the house's base – the cornerstone. I run my fingers over it. It feels cool and rough.

There's nothing there.

But it feels like there *should* be. I let my fingers fall. I want to cry with frustration. "Nate, what are you trying to tell me?" I whisper.

"Lost something?" a voice taunts.

I hold back a shriek and spin around. Nothing – only moonlit trees. Anger rushes through me, and I leap up. "I know that's you,

Sybil!" I snap. "Come out and fight! What's the matter? Are you scared?"

I sense the spirit's anger. Or am I just imagining it? But I know I didn't imagine that voice. I stare in front of me, trying to see her. My fists are so tight that my fingernails dig into my palms.

Then I jump as a window opens. A circle of light falls on me. "Who's there?" a sharp voice calls.

I stand frozen. It's the woman from before, holding up a flashlight. "You!" she cries when she sees me. "What are you doing here?"

"I – I'm sorry –" I gasp. "I thought I lost something –"

The woman jerks away from the window. A second later I hear, "Hello, police? This is Mrs Dumont!"

No! I stumble in the clumsy shoes as I race for the gate. As I run, I see the well. It looks just the same, even if the house doesn't. It's where we thought Sybil died.

My scalp crawls. How could we have been wrong? *How?* Her heart exploded – we saw it!

No time to think. I reach the fence and climb. My palms are so clammy that I almost slip. Then I'm on the other side again, pounding down the road.

❦ 6 ❦

I make it back to the Baxters' without anyone
seeing me. When I'm in the spare bedroom again
I pace back and forth, too nervous to sleep.

Sybil's returned. I'm positive now. What has
she *done*? Where's ... ?

Panic hits me as I realise I've forgotten his
name. I press my hands to my forehead. Frank?
Jake? Then it comes – *Nate*!

I sink down on to the bed and hug my arms.
'Nate,' I think. I repeat it to myself as hard as I
can. 'Nate, Nate.' Oh God, what's going on? Why
is it so hard to keep him in my head?

I jump as someone knocks. "Who is it?" I call.

The door opens. "Just me." Ruth slips in and
shuts the door behind her. Her long blond hair
is loose now, and her face looks more like Nate's

than ever. I stare at her, remembering what he looks like. I miss him so much it hurts.

"Are you all right?" Ruth asks. "I heard you pacing."

I shake myself. "I'm fine," I tell her. "Just a bad dream."

Ruth looks worried as she sits on the bed beside me. She clears her throat. "In fact ... I heard you sneak back into the house, too. Iris, are you *sure* nothing's wrong?"

I wince before I can help it. "I'm sure. I – I just had to go do something. Please don't say anything to your mother, OK?"

Ruth nods, her eyes wide. And I don't know why – maybe because she looks so much like Nate – but all of a sudden I can't hold it all inside me anymore.

I touch her arm. "Ruth, listen – everything *isn't* all right. It's so crazy – you're totally not going to believe me – but –"

"Go on," she says in a rush. "I'll believe you, I promise!"

So I tell her.

I tell her how, all my life, I've been having dreams of a boy. And in the dreams, we shared a love so strong that nothing else mattered.

"It turned out that those were memories," I tell her. I trace a pattern on the bedspread. "You see, Nate and I have spent life after life together. He's always been the one I love – always. This time, an evil spirit named Sybil had us born in different times, but we found each other anyway. But now –" I break off. For a second I can't go on.

"Now you're here in this time," Ruth finishes. Her face is white. "And Nate should be here too, but he isn't!"

I sag in relief. "You believe me?"

She nods so hard that her blond hair bounces. "It all makes sense! I've always felt like I *should* have a brother named Nate – that it wasn't a game when I pretended I did." Then she shivers.

"Oh, Iris, I think something must have gone very wrong. Do you think ... do you think maybe he died before he was born?"

I grasp her arms. "No, he's alive! He's 17; he's as real as you or me! I've –" I stop short before I say, 'I've touched him – kissed him – been held in his arms.'

Ruth looks like she knows what I was going to tell her. She squeezes my hand. "You're in love with my brother – that almost makes you my sister. I'll help you find him. Don't worry."

We talk for a long time. I tell her about the old house and how it's changed. "It has *got* to be the key," I say. "Only I don't know how."

"We'll find out!" The bed creaks as Ruth bounces up on her knees. "That cornerstone is a clue, I bet – it's why you felt drawn to it!"

"But there's nothing there." I shove my hands through my hair, frustrated. "I checked."

"Then we'll check again!" Ruth cries. She looks so excited.

"Remember what I told you about Sybil," I warn her. "And Mrs Dumont – the woman who owns the house. She called the police tonight. We've got to be careful! This isn't a game."

Ruth's smile fades. "I know that," she says. "It's the most serious thing in the world. I have to get my brother back." Then she studies me. "You know, I think you should go to sleep now."

I almost laugh. "How can I?"

"Because you need to dream," Ruth tells me. "You always saw Nate in your dreams before, right? So maybe you'll see him now, and he can tell you how to fix everything."

I bite my lip. I haven't told Ruth how Nate keeps fading from my mind. If I go to sleep, what if he fades away for good? But all of a sudden I have the terrible sense that time is running out – and that Nate, wherever he is, may not have much of it left.

The thought is like a punch to the stomach. 'Nate, I will *not* let you slip away,' I tell him. 'I'll do whatever it takes to find you again.'

I clench my fists. "OK," I say. "I'll try it."

⟐

"Iris! Iris, don't forget me! Hold on ... please hold on ..."

I wake up with a start. The voice is still ringing in my ears. It sounded like a boy a little older than me – someone who's almost a man. It would have been a nice voice, if he didn't seem so upset.

What a weird dream. I yawn and get out of bed. I can see out the window that it's late afternoon now – I've been napping most of the day. I stretch, feeling lazy and relaxed, and then I go over and gaze at myself in the mirror. My blouse is rumpled, my hair messy. "Oh, very attractive, Iris," I say out loud. I start to brush my hair in long, slow strokes.

The hairbrush is kind of funny. Old-fashioned – different from the ones in my own time. It's almost flat, and the bristles are softer. I stop and stare at it as the words hit me.

My own time?

It all rushes back. I don't belong here. Not without – not without – *who?*

I can't remember! And I know I have to – it's so important. More important than anything in my entire life. I sink down on to the bed again and clutch my head. '*Think*, Iris!' The dream – that voice – 'Don't forget me.'

"Nate!" I cry out. The relief as I remember is like cool water on a hot day. How can I keep forgetting him like this, how?

I struggle to recall what he looked like, and then I catch myself. No, not *looked* like – what he *looks* like. He still exists. He told me to hold on. But I can't see his face, no matter how hard I try.

Mrs Baxter's painting! I scramble up and rush into the hallway. A moment later I push open the door of the front room where she paints. She's not there – I can hear her in the kitchen.

The painting of the boy is gone.

∞ 7 ∞

On the easel is a new painting – the house down the road with its two grey towers. The sight of it chills me. Then I see a stack of canvases leaning against the wall and I pounce on them.

The painting of the boy is on top. "Nate," I murmur. I crouch down and gaze at him – his dark eyes, his rumpled sandy hair, his broad shoulders.

I'm so relieved I want to cry. "I miss you," I whisper. With a gentle finger, I touch the boy's face. "Nate, I'll find you again," I tell him. "I promise."

When I look at the other paintings, they're almost all of Nate. The very last ones show him a few years younger. I drink in his face, his smile. Mrs Baxter must have been painting him for a long time.

Then I hear footsteps, and turn as she comes in. "Oh good, you're awake," she says. "I looked in on you a few times, but you were dead to the world."

'Dead to the world.' Not a comforting phrase. Slowly, I stand up. "Why are you painting that house?" I ask.

Mrs Baxter's eyebrows arch. "Why ... I don't know. It just popped into my head this morning. Strange, isn't it?"

She frowns as she sits in front of the easel. She picks up her paintbrush, then sets it down. "Why *am* I painting this?" she mutters. "I don't even like the place."

"That boy you keep painting ..." I start.

Mrs Baxter winces. "Oh, don't say it," she bursts out. "I know it's crazy."

"That's not what I was going to say," I tell her in surprise.

"It wasn't?" She sighs. "Well, my husband thinks it's crazy. He says I have an obsession."

"Is that why he's gone all the time?"

I hadn't meant to ask. But the second I do, I know I'm right. Mrs Baxter's mouth tightens.

"He says he can't compete with a ghost boy," she says at last. "He thinks I'm not right in the head. But the boy haunts *him*, too!" she goes on in a rush. "I know he does. I've heard my husband dreaming, calling out 'My son!'"

I swallow. "Your son?"

Mrs Baxter looks so sad – so fragile. "Oh, now you *will* think I'm crazy," she whispers. "We've never had a son. But I feel as if ..." She trails off.

I go to her and touch her arm. "You're not crazy," I say in a soft voice.

She shakes her head and snatches up her paintbrush again. She starts to paint, not looking at me. "I'm very sorry to have said anything about it," she says. "Why, you hardly even know us! I don't know what you must think."

I long to tell her Nate *is* her son. The words won't come out – I can't stop staring at the painting. The house looks brand new, like it's just been built. Something about it feels important, like there's some detail that I'm missing.

But I don't know what.

All of a sudden I feel like there's less time than ever. "Did something happen at that house 18 years ago?" I blurt out.

Mrs Baxter freezes. The paint on her brush is a dark, greenish black. It glistens like oil. "Why do you ask that?" she says.

"Please, just tell me!" I beg. "You can trust me."

She sighs. "You know … I *do* trust you." She goes silent for a moment and stares at the painting. Then she puts the paintbrush down.

"It was hardly anything," she says at last. "But you see, when Mr Baxter and I were first married, we were so much in love – so tender with each other. And one night, we had a midnight picnic in a field not far from here. It was so pretty in the moonlight."

She stares down at her hands. Her cheeks redden. "We almost – well. I shouldn't say such things to a young girl. But things became ... romantic."

At first I'm not sure what she means. Then I remember that we're in 1922 and I get it. I go very still.

Mrs Baxter clears her throat. "But then – well, I glanced up and saw that old house." She shudders. "It seemed so menacing, as if it didn't want us there. I – I got scared. I just wanted to go home."

"So you did," I whisper.

She nods, looking miserable. "And it sounds crazy, but nothing has really been right since. It's as if we left something in that field that we needed very much, and we've never gotten it back."

I feel electric – all of a sudden the puzzle pieces fit together. *The house.* This is how it's the key! Nate was supposed to be conceived that night, but the house creeped his mother out and he wasn't. If it had been the right house – the one Nate and I knew – then that wouldn't have happened!

Then dread fills me. Does that mean Nate really *doesn't* exist? That can't be true! I dreamed he was calling me. Or did I only dream that because I wanted it to be real?

Mrs Baxter rises. "Anyway, I better go check on dinner," she says. I can see how embarrassed she is – how sad she feels. She hurries from the room.

I should go after her. Instead I stand there and stare at the painting. It shows the same corner of the house that I went to last night – where I felt drawn by the cornerstone, as if Nate were trying to tell me something.

And then I see what it is about the house that was bothering me. I gasp out loud. It's so obvious! Why didn't I think of it before?

Ruth bursts in, her face eager. "Iris, you're awake! Did you dream anything?"

I spin towards her. "We've got to go back to the old house! We've got to go *now*!"

Her eyes widen. "But – it's still light outside. What if the woman calls the police again?"

"I don't care! Hurry!" I grab her hand and we rush for the front door. When we reach the main road, we start to run.

⚛ 8 ⚛

'Hold on,' Nate says to himself. 'Hold on.'

He's been saying it for what feels like a long time. He doesn't know how long it's really been. A day? A week?

Maybe forever.

He feels so cold, even in the heat of the sun. He stares up at the house. It's only half built, but he can tell that it's all wrong. What are those two towers doing there? Maybe he's not where he thinks he is ... but then he looks around him again and sees the shape of the hills. Rufus the camel.

No, this is the right place. But Nate has walked down that road a dozen times now. His house isn't there.

And Iris is gone.

How could he have found her at last, only to lose her again so soon? *How?* Nate presses his hands to his head and struggles to picture her. It's gotten hard to do now, and his muscles clench with the effort. But then she comes to him – her long dark hair, her wide grey eyes and slim shape. The wary look on her face – her sudden smile.

The feel of her lips on his.

'We'll be together again,' Nate vows to her in his head. 'Iris, I promise you.'

All around him, workmen are busy building the wrong house. The air is full of the sound of hammers and saws – of the men shouting to each other. Nate knows by now that it's pointless, but he goes up to one of them anyway.

"Excuse me," he says. "Can you tell me what year it is?"

The man's wearing old-fashioned clothes and sawing a piece of wood. He glances up and for a second Nate catches his breath. But the worker looks past him to someone else. "Joe, can you help me with this?" he calls.

Nate clenches his fists. *"Listen to me!"* he cries. "I'm right here – I'm talking to you!"

Another man walks over to where Nate is standing. Nate jumps aside fast as the man passes. A few times now people have walked right *through* him. Nate hates to admit it to himself, but it scares him every time it happens. It's as if ...

"You're a ghost," a cheerful voice behind him says.

Nate spins to face it.

Ever since he jumped off the gate with Iris and found himself here, he's had the sense he's being watched. And he's had a terrible feeling that he knows exactly who is watching him.

Now she's standing in front of him.

"Sybil," Nate says in a low voice.

It's her, all right – the evil spirit who's been keeping him and Iris apart. She's only about the size of a toddler, and she wears a dress with a wide sash. She leers at him.

"Hello, Nate dear," she says.

Nate grits his teeth. "What the hell have you done? Where's Iris?"

Sybil plays with a strand of her long hair. "Oh, don't worry. Iris is just fine. Of course, she's having a hard time remembering *you* now."

The words are like a punch to the gut. Nate glares, refusing to show his pain. "I thought we killed you," he says.

Sybil giggles. "Oh, Nate, how sweet! Did you really think I need a *heart* to survive? I'm a spirit! You killed my ability to take on a physical body, that's all. I can survive quite well without one. And so can you, it seems," she adds with a smirk.

Nate stares at her as it all sinks in. 'You're a ghost.' That's what she'd said. For a second he can't speak.

Sybil puts her hands behind her back and walks around him, looking him up and down. "There doesn't seem to be much *to* you these days, does there?" she trills. "You're kind of dim around the edges."

Nate swallows. He's been trying not to think about it, but Sybil is right. He's faint – ghostly. He can see the grass right through one of his shoes.

All around them, the workmen keep on building. No one notices them.

"Of course, you're not really a ghost," Sybil says in a musing tone. "No, you're more like a memory."

"A memory." Nate's voice is hoarse.

"You see, you've never been born," she explains. "But somehow you're still holding on, aren't you? You refuse to just *die*." She snarls the last word with a flash of sharp, pointed teeth.

Nate feels even colder than before. He wants to think she's lying – but holy Moses, this would explain so much.

Sybil's eyes are pure black, her skin clammy white. A snake darts from her mouth, then vanishes again. "What I can't work out is what you're doing *here*," she hisses. "Clever boy – did you sense something was wrong? But you're in the wrong time, Natey-boy. It's too late."

"I didn't choose to come here," Nate retorts. His mind is racing. What has Sybil done? How did she make it so that he's never been born?

"Oh, you didn't choose on purpose," she says with a sweet smile. "But some part of you made it happen." She smirks. "And there's nothing you can do, that's the best part! Even if you work out –" She stops herself.

'Even if I work out what?' Nate thinks. He doesn't say it, and after a second Sybil goes on.

"Anyway," she gloats, "even if you existed again, the only thing that could get you and Iris back in the same time is down in that well. But not in *this* time."

She puts on a sad face. "Sorry, Nate – you're sunk. Because it's getting harder to hold on, isn't it?"

Her voice turns sing-song. "If you don't keep focused, you'll just fade away to nothing. Not much longer now! At least Iris won't miss you. Why, she can barely remember who you are."

Nate can't hold himself back any longer. "Tell me what you've done!" he shouts. "Where is she?" He lunges for Sybil ... but the spirit is gone.

∞

It's dark now and the workmen have left for the day. Nate sits against the side of the half-built house. He repeats the facts in his head, over and over: 'I am Nate Baxter. I was born in 1905. I'm in love with Iris. I am Nate Baxter. I was born in 1905. I'm in love with –'

"Iris," he whispers out loud. He rests his head against the house and for the hundredth time, tries to think. The year must be around 1870. Too late, Sybil said. If she's right and he somehow sent himself here on purpose – what was he hoping to do?

And oh, God, where's Iris?

From here, Nate can see the well. He's spent hours peering over its side, trying to see what Sybil might have meant. There's nothing there.

Then a thought comes to him. No matter what time Iris is in, it's likely she'll be in this same place too, isn't it? She'll be trying to find him! And if she's in the future – maybe he can leave her a message.

The workmen have left their tools behind. A hammer and chisel lie nearby. Nate reaches for them, but his fingers pass right through. *Damn!* He's just a memory, with no power of touch.

But ghosts are just a memory too, aren't they? And you hear stories about them moving things around. So maybe it's possible.

Nate stares at his fingers. His teeth grit together – he concentrates as hard as he can. At last a bit of colour flows into his hands. He can't see the ground through them anymore.

Yes! But keeping his hands this solid makes his muscles scream. He'd planned to leave a message on the well, but he'd never manage to carry the tools that far. Trembling with effort, Nate picks up the hammer and chisel and scratches a message on the cornerstone of the house.

When Nate finishes, he's weak. The tools slip from his grasp and he slumps against the house again, his thoughts spinning. He feels like smoke – as if he's about to drift away into nothing.

'I am Nate Baxter. I was born in ... in ...'

He can't recall. He has a sister, doesn't he? Or is it a brother? Nate presses his fists against his eyes, gasping, and knows that he's close to the end now.

'Iris, don't forget me!' he screams in his mind. 'Please, hold on!'

❧ 9 ❧

When Ruth and I reach the house, we sneak around to the side and peer in through the fence. I can see the cornerstone from here.

Only now I know that's *not* the cornerstone.

I explain to Ruth as fast as I can. "Your mother was painting the house this morning – the way it was when it was first built. See that big stone block? There's another one under it! So many years have passed that dirt's covered it all up."

Ruth's eyes are wide. "So?"

"There's something on that stone," I tell her. "I know there is."

She clutches my arm. "Something from Nate?"

I tell myself it's impossible – Nate was never even born! But I refuse to believe that, and my chin lifts. "I think so."

Ruth narrows her eyes at the house like a detective. If I weren't so worried, I'd want to laugh. "All right," she says. "I'd better go see."

"Ruth, no way! I'll go."

"Mrs Dumont will call the police if she sees you again!" Ruth reminds me. "But I'm only 12 years old. Here." She pulls a rubber ball out of her skirt pocket and bounces it. "I'll just say I was looking for this!"

I hate to admit it, but she's got a point. "All right," I say. "Hurry! And be careful."

She nods. I watch her climb over the fence and slip away through the orange trees. On the way, she steps over a ladder that the gardener must have left lying in the grass.

"Hurry, hurry," I murmur. My fists are clenched. I can't shake the feeling that we have to move *fast* – wherever Nate is, it might already be too late.

Ruth crouches down beside the corner of the house. She takes a rock and starts to dig in the dirt. When at last she uncovers the real cornerstone, my heart leaps. I knew it! She digs even harder, with both her hands – I can tell she wants to find Nate as much as I do.

"Please," I whisper.

All of a sudden Ruth seems to shudder. She stops for a moment.

I frown, ready to go see if she's OK – but then she starts to dig again. She brushes the stone clean with her palm and leans down to study it.

At last she walks back over. Her shoulders are slumped.

"What is it?" I burst out as she reaches the fence.

"There's nothing there," she says.

"*What?* There has to be!"

Ruth shrugs and climbs back over the fence. "There isn't."

My head feels like it's swimming. "I'd better go check."

She grabs my arm. "No, you can't! You'll get caught!"

"*You* didn't. Ruth, let go of me!" I try to shake her off. I can't believe how strong she is. Her grip tightens – her fingers feel like claws.

"*I said no!*" she hisses.

I freeze as I stare into her eyes. All of a sudden I'm dizzy. The world seems to slide sideways. She reminds me of someone ... but I can't think who.

What am I even doing here?

Ruth's eyes have gone so dark that I can't see her pupils. Her voice is like a cat's purr. "Iris, don't be silly," she says. "I've already checked. Besides, we need to get you home. You haven't been feeling well."

I swallow. "I haven't?"

She tucks her arm through mine. "No. You've been imagining people who don't exist, and I don't know what else! Mom said I should play along with you, but ..."

I don't know what to think. Maybe it's true. But wasn't I looking for someone? It seems so important, like I shouldn't leave just yet.

"Come along, Iris." Ruth is starting to sound angry. I take a step backwards, confused. This doesn't feel right. Those eyes. I've seen them before.

'Iris, don't forget me! Hold on!'

The voice seems to explode through my head. *Nate!* Everything becomes clear again. I have to find him. Time's running out!

"Iris?" Ruth says.

And then I know that it's not really Ruth at all. Sybil's gotten inside her – she's controlling her.

My skin feels like ice. I lick my lips and nod. "OK," I say. "You're probably right. I am kind of tired."

"Good girl." The Ruth-Sybil thing smiles, and I shudder. Her teeth look pointed.

I wait until she turns, then shove her as hard as I can. She stumbles and hits her head on a tree. She goes down like a sack of bricks and lies still, her face pale. For a second I'm panicked – have I killed Ruth? But then I see she's breathing.

I scramble over the fence and run for the corner of the house.

The message is old and worn, but when I kneel down I can still make out its letters. 'There's something in the well that can help us. Don't ever forget me. Nate.'

"Never!" I tell him in a fierce whisper. I race back across the grass and grab the wooden ladder. It's sunset now, and there are long shadows across the lawn. I don't care if I'm seen – I have to hurry, there may not be time.

I reach the well and slide the ladder into it. I clamber down. The familiar walls seem to press in on me – Nate and I were here once before, fighting Sybil. The bottom is muddy; it sucks at my shoes. I scramble around in it, not caring.

As if my hand is guided by the same instinct that led me to the message, I find two gemstones. I dig them out of the mud. One is green, and one is silver. They sparkle in the dim light.

I stare at them in my hand. Somehow I know that they're something to do with me and Nate. I shove them in my pocket and look up at the circle of sky. I've got to get out of here – if Sybil comes back, I'll be trapped.

I climb back up as fast as I can. I sigh with relief as I pull myself over the edge of the well and drop on to the grass. Then I freeze.

Mrs Dumont is standing there. And her eyes are pure black.

"You just couldn't leave it alone, could you?" she hisses. "You and *Nate* – always you and *Nate*!"

I try to run but she grabs me. She snatches the gemstones from my pocket. I shriek and try to get them back. We struggle. Oh God, she's so strong! Sybil has totally taken her over.

"You don't even know what these *are!*" she snarls.

"I know they're important!" I manage to get one of the stones and clench it in my fist. Then I cry out as she twists my arm behind my back. She still has the other stone – she throws it away into the shadows and bares her teeth at me.

"Well, let me fill you in," she says. "When you and Nate tried to kill me, you left little pieces of your souls in that well. They turned into those stones and joined together – until I separated them! For you to be in the same time, those stones have to be joined. If they're not, you can forget it – you'll never be together again."

I'm panting in pain and dismay. Is that true? It must be – that was why Nate told me to search the well! I've got to find the other stone!

Then Sybil smirks and twists my arm harder. "Of course, Nate's not in much shape to be with you even if he could be. And soon you won't be, either."

My heart leaps. "Is Nate still alive?" I start to ask. But I can't.

Because Mrs Dumont – Sybil – puts her hands around my neck and begins to squeeze.

Nate's only just hanging on. He's so tired, he hardly knows who he is. 'Iris,' he thinks weakly. He stares at the message he's scratched, praying it will do some good.

Then his gaze falls on the tools that he dropped, and all of a sudden he knows.

Of course! He came to this time because he had to stop the wrong house from being built! He doesn't know why it matters, but it does.

And the time to stop it would have been when the plans were changed – not now.

Nate's thoughts spin. He's just a ghost, a memory. Somehow he brought himself here – so can he go to other times, too?

The idea jolts him. Why didn't he think of it sooner? He longs to go to wherever Iris is, but he's fading fast. Soon he won't even know who she is anymore. His only hope is to try and change the house.

Then he hesitates. If he succeeds, will he exist again? He could be stuck in the past – and Sybil told them once that if he and Iris die in different times, they'll be separated forever. He knows it's true. He can sense it. Maybe he should just fade away, and let Iris forget about him.

His jaw hardens. *No.* He will not give up. She'll find his message – she'll work out what Sybil meant about the well. They *will* be together again.

Nate closes his eyes and thinks as hard as he can. 'I have to go to when the plans were changed.' He thinks it over and over, willing himself there.

At last he opens his eyes.

He's in the same spot. Only now it's an empty field, and it's daylight. A man and a woman stand talking nearby. The woman wears long skirts ... and has eyes of pure black.

Nate's fists clench. He feels dizzy, but he gets to his feet. He's still just a memory.

The man and woman don't see him. "Yes, it's a beautiful spot," the woman says. "Have I told you that I've changed my mind about the plans?"

The man blinks. "But Madam, my men are ready to start work tomorrow."

"Good. Tell them I want *this* house, instead." The woman pulls a piece of paper from her bag. "Here are the new plans."

Nate doesn't stop to think. He's pretty much a spirit too – if Sybil can enter people, so can he. He plunges into the woman. Sybil's there, cold and slimy-feeling. She gives a silent shriek of surprise.

"Fancy meeting you here," Nate says grimly. He wraps his spirit-self around her and drags her from the woman's body.

"Mrs Tyler? Are you all right?" the man asks.

"I ..." The woman stares down at the papers in her hand, looking dazed.

Sybil's in her little-girl form again, snarling and shrieking as she and Nate struggle. It's like battling smoke. Then she rushes right at Nate – and becomes part of him.

"Perfect," she hisses in his head. "I'll kill you first, then go back in time again and *still* change the plans!"

Nate winces. He can feel her latching on to every forgotten atom of him. She cackles with laughter as she tears the atoms wider and wider apart. Nate gasps as he begins to break into pieces – oh, God, he can't hold on much longer!

A snake flickers from Sybil's mouth. "Guess what? I can be in two times at once," she sneers. "And what's happening in Iris's time is *so* sad. Lucky me, I get to watch you both die!"

The words give Nate strength. "No!" he shouts. Before Sybil can react, he latches on to her in the same way she latched on to him. He starts to spread himself as thin as he can.

Sybil screams as she's pulled apart. The snakes go wild, waving from her mouth and eye sockets. "You won't do it!" she shrieks. "It will kill you, too!"

"Watch me," Nate says.

Mrs Tyler's eyes have turned a gentle brown. She shakes her head. "Why – whatever was I thinking? Why would I want this dreadful house when the one we've planned is so lovely?"

She tears the new plans up. At the same second, with a final burst of strength, Nate blows himself and Sybil to nothing.

Darkness.

⋘ 11 ⋙

It's all so sudden.

One moment I'm gasping, choking, struggling to breathe. All I can see are Sybil's black eyes as she squeezes the life from me. I can hear Ruth screaming, and I'm so relieved she's all right. 'Run!' I want to yell, but I can't get the words out.

Then everything changes.

A burst of energy roars past. It knocks me off my feet. Mrs Dumont vanishes. Ruth's screams stop like a tap that's been turned off.

I roll on to my side, coughing and clutching my neck. I can breathe! I gasp in big gulps of air. Nothing has ever tasted so good.

When I look up, my heart skips. The first old house is back again. It's abandoned, and it looks so friendly – like it's happy I'm there.

I stare at it as I get to my feet. The house isn't as run-down as in my time. I must still be in 1922, but there's no sign of Ruth now. Or Nate.

There's something clenched in my hand. I open my fist and look. The silver gemstone. Then it hits me. The other gem! Will it still be in the grass, or not?

"Please, please," I pray. I race over to where Sybil threw it. I drop to my knees and scrabble in the long grass. I feel panicked – without that gem, Nate and I will never be together again. Then I see a glint of emerald green. I give a cry of joy as my fingers close around the stone.

"Not so fast," a voice whispers.

I whirl around. At first I can't see anything ... but then I see a pair of *eyes*. No face, no body – just black eyes full of hatred, glaring at me.

"There may not be much of me left, but I can stop *this*, at least," the voice hisses. I shudder as coldness sweeps over me. She's trying to control me!

"No!" I grab the stone and scramble away. I can just see her following me, like a wisp of smoke in the sunlight.

"Leave us alone!" I shout. *"Die!"*

"You wish," Sybil's voice snarls. She rushes towards me. I fumble with the pair of stones, trying to work out how they fit together. There are two different ways – I don't know which is right!

Then I scream as coldness takes over my body. Thoughts that aren't mine beat into my brain. 'Throw the stones away! Destroy them!' the thoughts scream.

"Get out of me, you bitch," I pant.

I try to shove Sybil out with my mind. We struggle – I can feel her holding on to me and I push harder. All of a sudden I see a tiny wisp of smoke in front of my chest. It's part of Sybil! Without thinking, I drop the stones and make the sign of the cross in it with my fingers.

I scream as I feel her writhing inside me. I fall backwards but keep my fingers in a cross. Sybil leaves my body in a rush, screeching like a banshee. She twists and struggles in the air as the cross destroys her.

"I don't deserve this!" she howls.

"Oh, you so do," I mutter, gritting my teeth.

She dissolves like specks of dust on the wind. Her eyes fade last. They look pained, as if she can't believe this is happening.

A final shimmer, and then she's gone.

The day feels brighter. I gasp as my shoulders slump. She's really dead this time – I hope.

Nate. With a sob, I scrabble for the stones. At first I can't find them, and terror grips me. Then I see them, and I snatch them up. I don't know which way they fit together. I don't care anymore. I choose a way, and lock the two stones into one.

They join with a ripple.

I cry out and hide my head as another rush of energy hits. When I open my eyes ... everything's changed again. I can hear the distant sound of traffic. The old house is even more run-down now.

"Iris!" a voice calls.

❦ 12 ❧

I whirl around. Nate has fallen to his knees beside me and pulled me into his arms. I can't speak. I just hold him as hard as I can and try not to cry. His heart pounds against mine – his arms are strong and firm around me.

He's real. He's alive.

Nate strokes my hair as he clutches me to him. "I thought I'd never see you again," he tells me in a hoarse whisper.

I nod against his chest. My throat feels tight. "I know. Me too."

I pull away a little and kiss his cheeks, his neck, his jaw. He takes my face in his hands and his mouth finds mine. I wrap my arms around his neck. The kiss is long, deep – all I want is for it to never end.

At long last, our lips leave each other. I swallow and touch Nate's cheek. I can't stop looking at him. He's the most beautiful boy I've ever seen. Nate lets out a breath and rests his head against mine.

Neither of us speaks.

When we get to our feet we still have our arms around each other. I feel as if I'll never let go of him again, not even for a second. Nate gazes towards the front gate. In the fading sun we can see that it's falling down. His throat moves.

"Is this –?" he says, and stops.

I nod, staring at the gate. "We're in my time."

I explain about the stones. It's one stone, now. Nate turns it over in his hand. It gleams green and silver. You can't see the join anymore.

Nate keeps looking down at it. Then he closes his fingers into a fist, covering the stone.

"All right," he says. "The only thing that matters is that we're together."

But it's not all that matters, and we both know it. Oh God, his family were all so haunted when Nate hadn't even been born. What must things have been like for them when he *was* born, and then went missing forever?

I think of Ruth and Mrs Baxter – of Mr Baxter, on his endless lecture tours. My heart feels like a fist is squeezing it.

Nate clears his throat and looks around us. "It'll be dark soon," he says. "Maybe the best thing is for us to stay here for the night."

I know he must be wishing his family was still down the road. But of course they aren't – they lived there almost a hundred years ago. It's so hard to take in.

I nod, and squeeze his hand hard. "Come on," I say.

Inside the house, everything is just as I remember. It's shadowy, but it feels friendly.

There's a pack of matches on the fireplace, and some old bits of wood. Nate builds a fire, and soon the room has a golden glow. We drag the sofa over near the fireplace and curl up on it.

Nate puts his arms around me and I snuggle against him. He bows his head against my shoulder. "It feels so good to hold you again," he says in a low voice.

My eyes are closed. My face is pressed against his neck. "I missed you," I whisper. His skin feels warm against my lips. "I missed you so much."

There's still such a lot we should tell each other. Nate has no idea yet what happened to me. I don't know what happened to him. But somehow, we don't say any of it. Not yet.

We just hold each other.

After a long time, I open my eyes. Nate and I are lying on the sofa. My head's on his chest, and I can hear the thud of his heart. I must have fallen asleep in his arms. I sit up a little and study his face in the firelight.

He's still sleeping, but I can't help myself. I trace my finger down his cheek. He has faint golden stubble that feels prickly. I love it.

Nate stirs and opens his eyes. His smile when he sees me makes me feel like someone just handed me the sun.

"Hello, beautiful girl," he says.

"Hi," I murmur back. I smile, too. "I've never slept with a boy before," I tell him. Then my cheeks redden as I realise what I've just said. When I said 'slept' I meant 'rested'.

Nate's cheeks redden a little, too, but he grins. "I'm glad to be the first," he says. "And only."

"And only," I agree. I stroke his sandy hair. "I don't think I'll ever want to sleep without you again."

Nate kisses me softly. "What a hardship. But I suppose I'll manage."

It's still dark outside, and I'm glad. I don't want to have to move. I want to lie here in Nate's arms forever. We've put the stone up on the mantelpiece. In the firelight it has an odd greenish glow.

I frown a little as I gaze at it. I want so much to believe that the nightmare is over now – that Nate and I are really together for good.

Then I bite my lip. Even if we are ... what are we going to do? I'm a runaway without a home. We'll have to lie about our ages, I guess, and hope that we can get jobs. And will Nate be OK? His time was so peaceful. What will he think about this strange new century, with its computers and cell phones and TV sets?

Nate touches my forehead. "You're worrying about something," he says.

"Kind of," I admit. "It's just that ... things in my time might be pretty different for you."

Nate's eyes are so brown. So warm. He grips my fingers.

"It's our time now," he tells me. "I can take whatever it throws at me – as long as I've got you."

I nod. I know it's true – I know how capable Nate is. It might be hard, but he'll be OK.

"I'm fine, too," I say. "As long as I've got you." I trace my finger over Nate's mouth, and he takes my hand and kisses it. The fire snaps and crackles.

Then I smile as I remember something. "Hey – what's 'Nate' short for, anyway?"

Our books are tested
for children and young people by
children and young people.

Thanks to everyone who consulted on
a manuscript for their time and effort in
helping us to make our books better
for our readers.

◈ About the Author ∂

Lee Weatherly was born in the USA in Little Rock, Arkansas. She was the youngest of three children and grew up in a house full of books. She always wanted to be a writer but had lots of other jobs first. Her favourite job was as a hostess at a ski resort – despite the fact she didn't know how to ski. She is very happy to be a writer now so she can work from home in her pyjamas if she wants to!

Lee has lived in the UK for almost 20 years. She lives in Hampshire with her husband and cat and goes for long walks and reads a lot. She's always been interested in Los Angeles and the idea of time travel ... so she couldn't resist writing about Iris and Nate, and thanks Barrington Stoke for making it happen.